Mog's
Amazing Birthday
Caper

Judith Kerr

COLLINS

For Tom, Tacy and Matthew

William Collins Sons & Co Ltd
London · Glasgow · Sydney · Auckland
Toronto · Johannesburg

First published by William Collins Sons & Co Ltd 1986
© text and illustrations Kerr-Kneale Productions Ltd 1986

Kerr, Judith
Mog's Amazing Birthday Caper
I. Title
823'.914 [J]   PZ7
ISBN 0-00-195557-8

All rights reserved. No part of this publication
may be reproduced, stored in a retrieval system,
or transmitted, in any form or by any means,
electronic, mechanical, photocopying,
recording or otherwise,
without the prior permission of
William Collins Sons & Co Ltd,
8 Grafton Street, LONDON W1X 3LA.

Printed and bound in Great Britain
by William Collins Sons & Co Ltd, Glasgow

Aa

Mog accidentally ate an alligator
and all were amazed at the . . .

. . . BANG!

Bb

Boohoo!

"You clumsy cat!   You crushed the cake and candles!"

Mog creeps off . . .

Cc

crossly . . .   to a corner . . .   for a catnap.

Dd

She dreams and dreams and dreams.
She dreams of dragons doing damage in the dark . . .

E e

. . . and elephants eating Emily . . .

Ff

... and her family floating far into a fog.

G g   Goodness!   A giraffe in the garden.

Hh

Mog
hisses
and
he
hops
into
a
helicopter.

Ii

"May I invite you to an ice cream?"
inquires an Indian.

Jj

A jaguar joins them with a jug of jelly . . .

K k

. . . to eat with a kipper and
ketchup from the kettle.

Ll

But look who is lurking!
Lying low!   Licking lips!   It's . . .

Mm

A monster !

Nn

"Don't nip my nose, you nightmare nibbler!"

It has not noticed Nicky with his net.

Oo

Oh!   Ooh!   Oops!

Outwitted!

Outraged!

Overpowered!

P p

Mog purrs, and they paddle past palm trees and parrots to a pale pink palace with purple pillars.

Q q

But what is that queer quiver?
A quake!   An earthquake!
"I feel quite queasy,"
says the queen.

Rr

The raging river rises round them.
"Run!" she roars.   "My royal rug will rescue us."

S s

Soaring into the sky, Mog sees
survivors struggling on a sinking sofa,
surrounded by smiling sharks.

T t

They're terrified!
They're Mr and Mrs Thomas!
They teeter, totter, trip,
their treacherous transport tilts . . .

Uu

Unbalanced!

Upset!

Upended!

Underwater

V v

But on the verge of vanishing for ever
Mog hears a voice,
first vague, then very vivid . . .

"Why are your whiskers wet?
What is this water?
Wake up!   We're on our way
to somewhere wonderful!"

Ww

X x

Mog goes on an extremely

She examines an axolotl . . .

exciting expedition.

and exclaims at an ox.

She yawns at a yak,
and then – yippee!   Yummy! . . .

Z z

Out of the zigzag zip-bag zooms something to guzzle,